BRAVE
Charlotte

For you, who else? — H.W.

For Nina . . . — A.S.

Text copyright © 2005 by Anu Stohner
Illustrations copyright © 2005 by Henrike Wilson
Translation copyright © 2005 by Alyson Cole
Translated from the original German by Alyson Cole

Typeset in Sabon
Art created with acrylics on cardboard

Published by Bloomsbury Publishing, New York, London, and Berlin
Distributed to the trade by Holtzbrinck Publishers

Library of Congress Cataloging-in-Publication Data
Stohner, Anu.
[Schaf Charlotte. English]
Brave Charlotte / by Anu Stohner ; illustrated by Henrike Wilson.—1st U.S. ed.
p. cm.
Summary: A headstrong sheep rescues the flock when their shepherd is injured.
ISBN-10: 1-58234-690-9 • ISBN-13: 978-1-58234-690-8
[1.Sheep—Fiction.] I. Wilson, Henrike, ill. II. Cole, Alyson. III. Title.
PZ7.S8699Bra 2005   [E]—dc22   2005045312

First U.S. Edition 2005
Printed in China by South China Printing Co., Dongguan, Guangdong
7 9 10 8 6

Bloomsbury Publishing, Children's Books, U.S.A.
175 Fifth Avenue, New York, NY 10010

All papers used by Bloomsbury Publishing are natural, recyclable products
made from wood grown in well-managed forests. The manufacturing processes
conform to the environmental regulations of the country of origin.

BRAVE
Charlotte

by Anu Stohner

illustrated by Henrike Wilson

BLOOMSBURY

NEW YORK BERLIN LONDON

Nobody knew why Charlotte was different from all the other sheep, but she had been different right from the start. When all the other lambs just stood shyly by their mothers . . .

... Charlotte was leaping
around, ready for an adventure.

Jack, the old sheep dog, tried
to keep Charlotte in line, but she
wasn't scared of him.

One day Charlotte went missing. The shepherd found her up a tree. Jack tried to chase her down, but Charlotte wanted to stay up there a little longer, and moved only when she was ready.

"*Tut, tut, tut,*" said the old sheep, shaking their heads disapprovingly. "Where is this all going to end?"

But that was just the beginning. Another time, Charlotte jumped over the side of a riverbank and went for a swim in the fast-running stream.

"*Tut, tut, tut,*" said the older sheep,
shaking their heads.
"*Tut, tut, tut.*"

Before long, Charlotte was up to more mischief. She had climbed to the very top of the highest peak— something no sheep had ever done before!

"Oh, oh, oh!" groaned the other sheep. They were hardly able to watch because it made them feel dizzy.

When they found Charlotte on the side of a dangerously busy road, staring at the oncoming traffic, all the sheep wanted to know what she was doing. But Charlotte didn't want to tell them.

"Oh my goodness!" exclaimed the old sheep. "What is she up to?"

What would they say if they knew that at night Charlotte secretly roamed through the countryside?

When all the others were sleeping, she would quietly slip away to her special place and gaze at the moon. Even Jack didn't notice anything out of the ordinary. But he didn't have very good ears these days.

Then, in autumn, as the days grew shorter and the nights darker, something terrible happened. The shepherd fell over and broke his leg. Jack barked and circled around him, but that didn't help one bit. The shepherd lay in the grass, not knowing what to do.

"Oh dear, oh dear, oh dear," said the older sheep. "Somebody must go to the farmer's house in the valley and get help."

"Jack should go. He is the only one who knows the way."
"But it is too far. He hardly even manages with the herd these days."
"Yes, that's true," said the others, shaking their heads in despair.

Then Charlotte said, "I'll do it. I'll go."
"Charlotte?" muttered the older sheep.
"The little rascal?"
"Out of the question!"
"A sheep has never gone to the valley alone."
"Absolutely not!"

The older sheep were beside themselves with worry, but Charlotte could no longer hear them. She had already reached the big oak tree and was trying to find the right way to the valley.

She bounded over fields,

through the fast-running stream,

and over the mountain tops,

until it got dark.